ZELF

THE CHRISTMAS ELF

by Mike Donahue

illustrated by Dan St John

WILDBASIN

P U B L I S H I N G

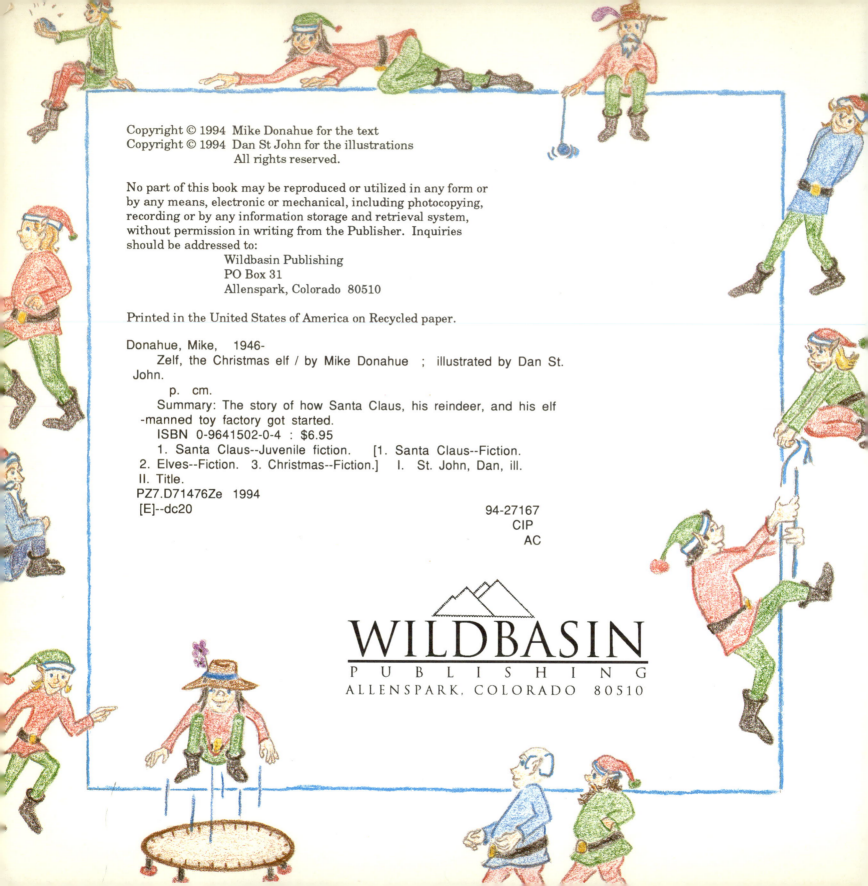

Donahue, Mike,   1946-
     Zelf, the Christmas elf / by Mike Donahue   ; illustrated by Dan St.
John.
        p. cm.
     Summary: The story of how Santa Claus, his reindeer, and his elf
-manned toy factory got started.
     ISBN 0-9641502-0-4 : $6.95
     1. Santa Claus--Juvenile fiction.   [1. Santa Claus--Fiction.
2. Elves--Fiction. 3. Christmas--Fiction.]   I. St. John, Dan, ill.
II. Title.
PZ7.D71476Ze 1994
[E]--dc20
                                                          94-27167
                                                             CIP
                                                             AC

WILDBASIN
P U B L I S H I N G
ALLENSPARK, COLORADO 80510

This Book Belongs To:

_____

Way back when old people were young, two very opposite old men lived far to the north in the land of cold and snow.

One, a very plump, round-faced fellow, hated the long cold winters. With nothing to do, he sat day after day rocking in front of his big fireplace.

" If I had just one wish, it would be to turn a cold winter day into the most exciting day of the year," he mumbled to himself as he fell asleep.

The slow rocking of his rocking chair sent the old man off into a wild dream.

In his dream he saw cold-toed boys and girls going off to bed, shivering under their blankets, and dreading waking up to another freezing winter day.

The white-haired gentleman's cheery wife watched as her sleeping husband's face went from a deep frown to a big, happy grin.

Then, like a burst of popcorn, the old man flew awake with such a start that he fell out of his rocking chair and rolled across the floor.

Unable to move quickly enough, he blurted out, "Cheery wife, you've got to make me a lively looking red suit and a big, strong bag that I can carry over my shoulder!"

His cheery wife smiled to herself and began sewing the big red suit. The round, jolly husband began sawing wood, pounding nails, and painting all kinds of fun looking toys.

Each day the jolly, bearded man worked faster and harder, but no matter how hard and how fast he worked, it wasn't fast enough. . . he could not make enough toys.

Little did they know that out near their wood pile, in a secret sort of place, lived a little, tiny, skinny elf and his happy, smiling wife.

The little, tiny, skinny elf had noticed that all of a sudden the lights in the nearby house were glowing far into the night, night after night.

With nothing better to do, curiosity drew the thin little fellow up to the window for a peek in to see what was going on in the big house.

Night after night he watched through
the window as his neighbor hammered,
painted, and made big piles of toys.

Then, one night he saw the old man sitting by
the fire, his head hung low, and a very dejected and
sad face staring at the blank floor.

Being a magical sort, the elf listened to the old man's sad thoughts.

Racing back to his own warm happy home, he excitedly explained to his merry wife, "I now know why our neighbor is up every night building toys. But he can't make enough. We need to help him!"

Inside the big house a tiny but firm knock brought the
cheery wife to open the door. "Who could possibly be out on such
a horribly cold night as this?" she said to herself.

Seeing nobody, she started to close the door. Being just a couple of hands high, the skinny little man called out: "Down here! We came to help your husband build his toys."

The surprised lady opened the door for the two little people. Walking over to the sad old man, the skinny little fellow stood very straight and spoke out, "Come on, we have work to do!"

The startled gentleman jumped in his seat,
looked down, squinted his eyes, rubbed them,
and squinted some more.

Once again the little fellow said, "Come on,
we have work to do!!"
At last, the puzzled old man said, "Who are
you and what are you talking about?"

"I'm your neighbor, Zelf. I live out near your wood pile in a special sort of place. I'm here to help you make the toys for all the boys and girls."

"I was looking in your window and listening to your sad thoughts. I like your idea and want to help you. Now, come on, we have lots of work to do."

"Ho, Ho!" chuckled the round gentleman, and with that he dropped his sad face, picked up his jolly laughter and bounded back to his work bench to begin making toys once again.

Like magic, Zelf touched a piece of wood. It
turned into a doll, a wagon, or a rocking horse.

While Zelf and his jolly friend made toys, the
two happy wives baked cookies and goodies to eat.

But even with Zelf's help, they couldn't make enough toys. The plump, round man found his sad, sad face once again.

Zelf just grinned, went to the door, gave a long shrill whistle and then went back to work.

A few minutes later another little, but solid knock
sent the cheery wife to see who was at the door.

In marched twenty-two of the funniest looking
little elves, all no bigger than Zelf and his smiling wife.

One at a time, each little elf came up to the round-faced gentleman, gave a deep bow and said, "Hello, Santa Claus. I am here to help you."

After the last little elf had bowed and gone off to work, the plump man turned to Zelf and said, "Santa Claus? What do they mean?"

"In elf language, Santa Claus means 'One Who Thinks of Others.' That is your new name," said Zelf.

Soon, all the toys were finished and stuffed into the big bag, ready for Santa Claus to deliver.

"**Oh No!**" exclaimed Santa. "I forgot to think of a way to haul all of these toys to the boys and girls!"

Without saying a word, some of the little
elves began making a big sleigh for Santa
Claus. . .

. . .while the others went out to find some friendly reindeer.

In less than a moment, the sleigh was ready, and the reindeer were harnessed. As one last surprise, Zelf called to Santa, "Crack your whip, point your arm, and the reindeer will fly through the air from rooftop to rooftop."

And so, with a crack of his whip and a point of his arm, Santa, his toys, and his reindeer sailed out of the north, and to the most exciting day of the year came Santa Claus, a "Ho Ho Ho," and a great big. . .

MERRY CHRISTMAS!!!

THE END.